T4-ADO-808

Date: 7/28/16

J 599.332 MAR
Markovics, Joyce L.,
Hedgehog /

PALM BEACH COUNTY
LIBRARY SYSTEM
3650 SUMMIT BLVD.
WEST PALM BEACH, FL 33406

by Joyce Markovics

Consultant: Thane Maynard, Director
Cincinnati Zoo and Botanical Garden
Cincinnati, Ohio

New York, New York

Credits

Cover, © Mr. SUTTIPON YAKHAM/Shutterstock; TOC, © Mr. SUTTIPON YAKHAM/Shutterstock; 4–5, © Mr. SUTTIPON YAKHAM/Shutterstock; 6T, © sso4in/Shutterstock; 6B, © Timmary/Shutterstock; 7, © blickwinkel/Alamy; 8, © Miroslav Hlavko/Dreamstime; 9, © FamVeld/Shutterstock; 10, © Africa Studio/Shutterstock; 11, © davemhuntphotography/Shutterstock; 12, © Ondrej Prosicky/Shutterstock; 13, © Arco Images GmbH/Alamy; 14, © DenisNata/Shutterstock; 15T, © David Glassey/Alamy; 15M, © Robert HENNO/Alamy; 15B, © Aleksandar Grozdanovski/Shutterstock; 16–17, © Eric Isselee/Shutterstock; 18, © sabyna75/Shutterstock; 19, © Miroslav Hlavko/Shutterstock; 20T, © Best dog photo/Shutterstock; 20B, © Best dog photo/Shutterstock; 21, © imageBROKER/Alamy; 22T, © rixonline/iStock; 22M, © senorjackson/iStock; 22B, © Steve Lovegrove/Shutterstock; 23TR, © Erni/Shutterstock; 24TR, © Ondrej Prosicky/Shutterstock; 24BL, © davemhuntphotography/Shutterstock; 24BR, © Flo-Bo/Shutterstock.

Publisher: Kenn Goin
Senior Editor: Joyce Tavolacci
Creative Director: Spencer Brinker
Design: Debrah Kaiser
Photo Researcher: Olympia Shannon

Library of Congress Cataloging-in-Publication Data

Markovics, Joyce L., author.
 Hedgehog / by Joyce Markovics.
    pages cm. — (Weird but cute)
 Audience: Ages 4–9.
 Includes bibliographical references and index.
 ISBN 978-1-62724-846-4 (library binding) — ISBN 1-62724-846-3 (library binding)
 1. Hedgehogs—Juvenile literature. I. Title.
 QL737.E753M37 2016
 599.33'2—dc23

2015011929

Copyright © 2016 Bearport Publishing Company, Inc. All rights reserved. No part of this publication may be reproduced in whole or in part, stored in any retrieval system, or transmitted in any form or by any means, electronic, mechanical, photocopying, recording, or otherwise, without written permission from the publisher.

For more information, write to Bearport Publishing Company, Inc., 45 West 21st Street, Suite 3B, New York, New York 10010. Printed in the United States of America.

10 9 8 7 6 5 4 3 2 1

Contents

Hedgehog 4

More Spiky Animals 22

Glossary 23

Index 24

Read More 24

Learn More Online 24

About the Author 24

What's this weird but cute animal?

Spiky!

It's a hedgehog.

Small, round body!

Some hedgehogs can fit in your hand.

Others are as big as soccer balls!

There are 17 different kinds of hedgehogs.

Where do hedgehogs live?

They live all over the world.

Sometimes, they make their homes in people's backyards!

Some people keep hedgehogs as pets.

Hedgehogs have sharp spikes called quills or spines.

The spines cover their bodies.

The spines help keep hedgehogs safe.

fox

If a **predator** attacks a hedgehog, it will get poked. Ouch!

To stay extra safe, hedgehogs use **poison**!

They chew poisonous plants and then lick their spines.

A hedgehog can have around 5,000 spines!

This might help keep predators away.

spines

Hedgehogs eat mostly insects.

They use their long noses to sniff out **prey** in the dirt.

Then they dig it up using strong, curved claws.

worm

Hedgehogs aren't picky eaters. They will also eat worms, eggs, and snails.

snail

egg

15

Grunt, grunt, grunt.

That's not a pig—it's a hedgehog!

Hedgehogs make pig-like grunts.

Hedgehogs make other noises, too. They huff, chirp, and hiss.

16

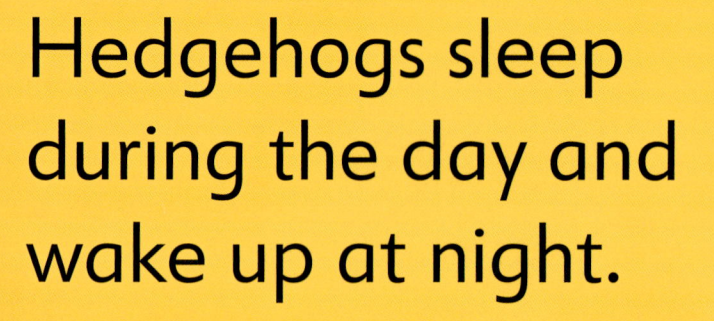

Hedgehogs sleep during the day and wake up at night.

They curl up into spiny balls as they sleep.

Sweet dreams!

Hedgehogs also curl up if they are in danger.

Baby hedgehogs have short, soft spines.

baby hedgehog

As they get older, their quills get longer and harder!

Baby hedgehogs are called hoglets.

More Spiky Animals

Echidna
Echidnas (ih-KIHD-nuhz) are small **mammals** that live in Australia. They are covered with short spines and have long, thin beaks. Unlike most mammals, echidna moms lay eggs.

Porcupine
A porcupine has soft fur mixed with sharp quills. If another animal attacks a porcupine, the porcupine's quills can loosen and get stuck in the predator's body!

Thorny Dragon
Thorny dragons are lizards that live in Australia. Their bodies are covered with hard spikes that look like thorns on a rose stem. They can also change the color of their skin!

Glossary

mammals (MAM-uhlz) warm-blooded animals that have hair or fur and drink their mothers' milk

poison (POI-zuhn) a substance that can harm or kill animals

predator (PRED-uh-ter) an animal that hunts and eats other animals

prey (PRAY) an animal that is hunted and eaten by another animal

Index

babies 20–21
claws 14
digging 14
food 14–15

noises 16
nose 14
poison 12–13
predators 10–11, 22

prey 14–15
size 6
sleep 18–19
spines 10–11, 12–13, 18, 20, 22

Read More

Dunn, Mary R. *Hedgehogs (Pebble Plus: Nocturnal Animals).* Mankato, MN: Capstone (2011).

Rissman, Rebecca. *Hedgehogs: Nocturnal Foragers.* Chicago: Heinemann (2015).

Learn More Online

To learn more about hedgehogs, visit
www.bearportpublishing.com/WeirdButCute

About the Author

Joyce Markovics is a writer who lives in Ossining, New York. As a small child, she dreamt of having tea with Mrs. Tiggy-Winkle, a fictional hedgehog created by Beatrix Potter.